Pat Hutchins

Greenwillow Books
An Imprint of HarperCollinsPublishers

Library of Congress Cataloging-in-Publication Data
Hutchins, Pat
  Don't forget the bacon! / by Pat Hutchins.
      p.   cm.
  "Greenwillow Books."
  Summary: A little boy goes grocery shopping for his mother and tries hard to
remember her instructions.
  ISBN 0-688-80019-X — ISBN 0-688-84019-1 (lib. bdg.)
  ISBN 0-688-06787-5 (1987 Printing)
  ISBN 0-688-06788-3 (lib bdg. 1987 Printing) — ISBN 0-688-08743-4 (pbk.)
  [1. Stories in rhyme]   I. Title.
PZ8.3.H965Do   75-17935
[E]   CIP
                                                                     AC

For Ben and Jeb Kidd

a cape for me?

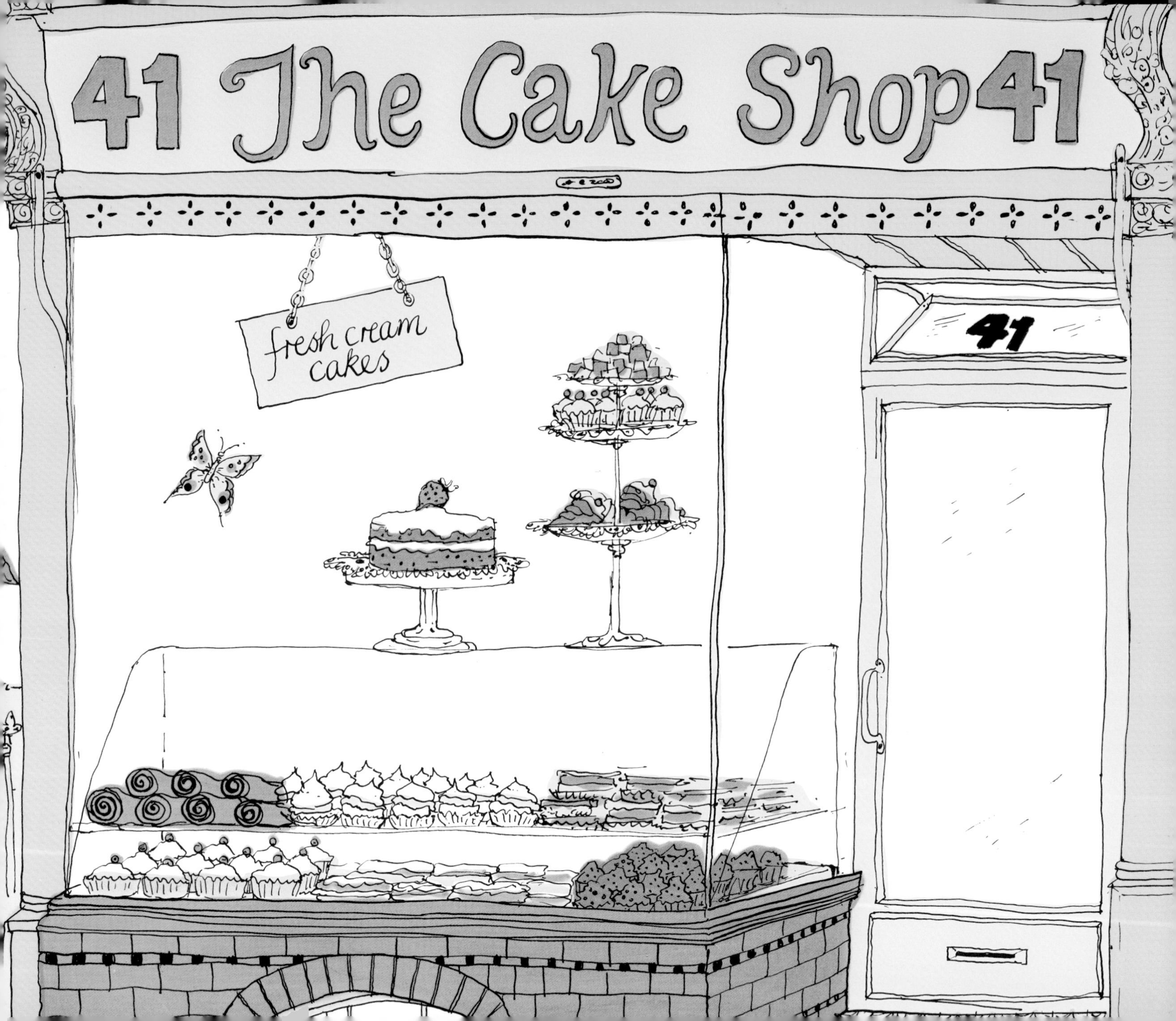
41 The Cake Shop 41
fresh cream cakes
41